Let's Learn Aesop's Fables

The Hare and the Tortoise

WINDMILL BOOKS

Published in 2018 by Windmill Books, an Imprint of Rosen Publishing | 29 East 21st Street, New York, NY 10010
Copyright © 2018 Windmill Books | All rights reserved. No part of this book may be reproduced in any
form without permission in writing from the publisher, except by a reviewer. | Illustrator: Monika Filipina

CATALOGING-IN-PUBLICATION DATA
Title: The hare and the tortoise.
Description: New York : Windmill Books, 2018. | Series: Let's learn Aesop's fables
Identifiers: ISBN 9781499483734 (pbk.) | ISBN 9781499483680 (library bound) | ISBN 9781499483581 (6 pack)
Subjects: LCSH: Fables. | Folklore.
Classification: LCC PZ8.2.A254 Har 2018 | DDC 398.2--dc23

Manufactured in China.
CPSIA Compliance Information: Batch BS17WM: For Further Information contact Rosen Publishing, New York, New York at 1-800-237-9932

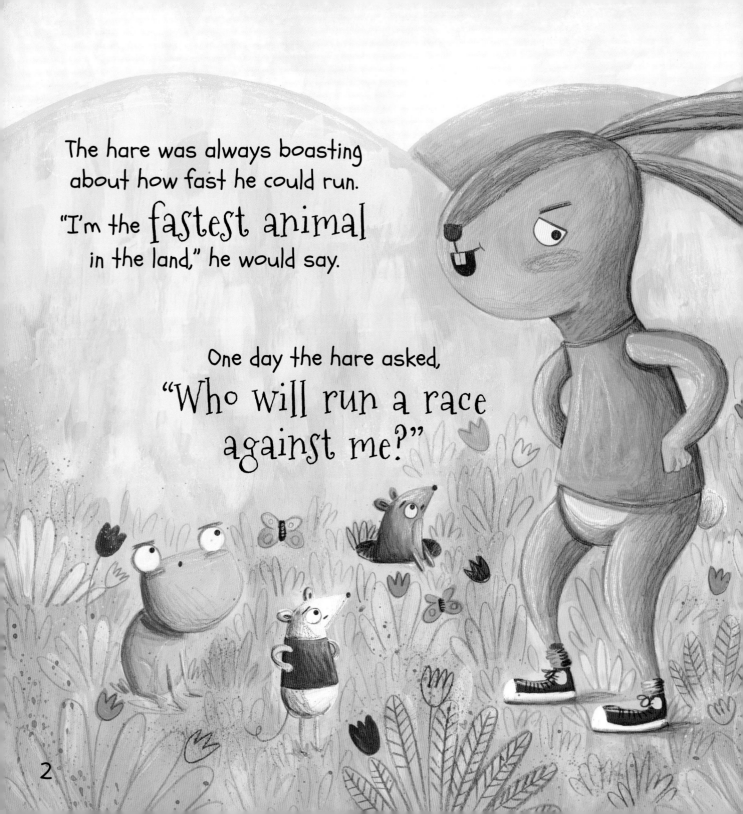

The hare was always boasting about how fast he could run.

"I'm the fastest animal in the land," he would say.

One day the hare asked, "Who will run a race against me?"

2

The other animals were fed up with the hare's boasting, but no one would accept his challenge because they were afraid of losing...

...no one except the tortoise.

3

"Ha ha!"

The hare laughed
out loud. The other
animals gasped.

The tortoise just smiled.

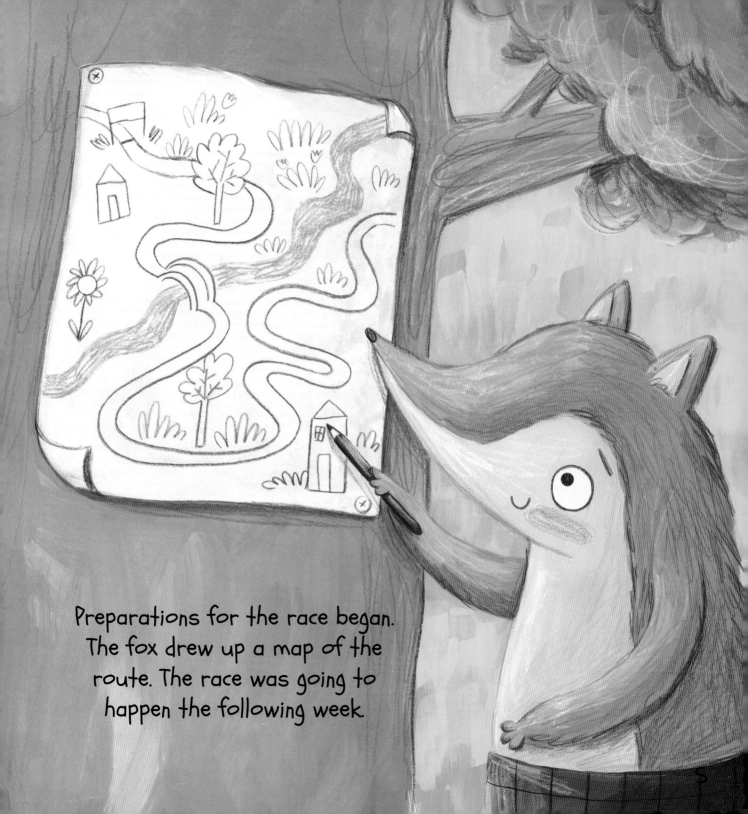

Preparations for the race began. The fox drew up a map of the route. The race was going to happen the following week.

Whoosh!

For the next seven days the hare showed off,
speeding around the meadow,
dashing up hills,
knocking animals over,
and upsetting just about everyone.

6

The tortoise just watched from afar as he chewed leisurely on grass and leaves.

The night before the race, the tortoise went to bed early, smiling happily as the sun went down.

"Early to bed, early to rise," he said to himself.

SHHH!

Meanwhile, the hare stayed up late partying with his neighbors, the badgers.

Their noisy antics kept everyone awake.

9

The next day dawned **bright and sunny.**

The tortoise awoke refreshed and full of energy. He ate a hearty breakfast then got ready for the race.

10

The hare wasn't feeling quite so refreshed. His late night meant he had hardly slept at all.

He felt exhausted.

He poured himself a large glass of carrot juice and yawned loudly.

11

Out in the meadow, the animals were gathering for the race.

There were stalls selling cakes and sandwiches. Balloons and banners had been tied to trees.

It was starting to feel like a party!

At last it was time for the race to start.

Feeling more like his usual self, the hare took his place at the start line.

"Get ready to lose!" he said to the tortoise.

The tortoise just smiled. He didn't seem in the least bit worried.

Then the fox began the countdown to the race.

"On your marks... Get set..."
The whistle blew, and they were off!

15

The hare dashed away at full speed around the meadow, then up the hill. He stopped to look back and saw the tortoise plodding along far behind.

Grinning happily, the hare
did a little dance on the hilltop.

16

As he ran down the hill, the hare grabbed some crunchy lettuce from a field. He stopped for a mid-morning snack.

Yummy!

The sun was warm and he decided to have a short nap. After all, he'd had a late night, and the tortoise was far behind.

17

In the meantime, the tortoise carried on.
He went up and over the hill.

18

ZZZZZ

He saw the hare snoozing under
a tree and marched bravely past.

The hare didn't stir a whisker.

19

Much, much later, feeling
stiff and cold, the hare
woke up with a start.

He looked up at the
sun and saw how low it
was in the sky. It must
be almost evening!
He feared the worst.

20

Pant!

Wheeze!

The hare flew around the rest of the route at top speed. He ran like he'd never run before.

But in the distance he heard shouting and clapping. He could just make out the tortoise nearing the finish line.

21

With the finish line in sight and
the crowd roaring him on, the tortoise
staggered on as fast as he could.

A few minutes later,
he crossed the line to
huge applause and
the crowd shouting his name.

23

The hare had lost his
own challenge.

From now on, perhaps he
wouldn't be so boastful.

Slow and steady
wins the race.

24